T0207990

The Colors of Spring

KK. GIGGLES

Illustrated by Abigail Z. Moore

To order additional copies of this book, contact:
Xlibris
844-714-8691
www.Xlibris.com
Orders@Xlibris.com

ISBN: Softcover   978-1-6698-5011-3
         EBook   978-1-6698-5007-6

Print information available on the last page

Rev. date: 09/30/2022

The Colors of Spring

Oh how I love the colors of spring.

Green grass, green trees, and red, yellow, purple flowers blooming.

Oh how I love the colors of spring.

Blue skies, white clouds, and rainbows.

Oh how I love the colors of spring.

Green frogs, brown squirrels, red robins, blue hummingbirds, black and red woodpeckers.

Oh how I love the colors of spring.

Red strawberries, orange oranges, pink grapefruit, green kiwi, and red, yellow, and green apples.

Oh how I love to eat the colors of spring.

Look at all the beautiful colors of spring!

Oh how I love the colors of spring.

"Now I can wear my colorful shirt and blue pants," said Aleu.

Oh how I love the colors of spring.

Now we can all wear the colors of spring.

"That's right," said Kyra.

"No more jackets!" said Leo with excitement.

Oh how I love the colors of spring!

Maybe it's time for me to bring out my rain boots, as she looked out the window.

What do you like about spring?

What would you wear?

What fruit would you eat?

I hope you enjoyed reading *The Colors of Spring*. Springtime is a beautiful time to watch nature change.

—K. K. Giggles

Printed in the United States
by Baker & Taylor Publisher Services